PLAYTALES

SLEEPING BEAUTY

Moira Butterfield

Heinemann

First published in Great Britain in 1997 by Heinemann Children's Reference,
an imprint of Heinemann Educational Publishers,
Halley Court, Jordan Hill, Oxford, OX2 8EJ,
a division of Reed Educational & Professional Publishing Ltd.

MADRID ATHENS PRAGUE WARSAW FLORENCE PORTSMOUTH NH
CHICAGO SAO PAULO SINGAPORE TOKYO MEXICO MELBOURNE
AUCKLAND IBADAN GABORONE JOHANNESBURG KAMPALA NAIROBI

ISBN 0 431 08142 5 Hb   ISBN 0 431 08147 6 Pb

A CIP catalogue record for this book is available at the British Library.

Co-author: Robin Edwards
Editor: David Riley
Art Director: Cathy Tincknell
Designer: Anne Sharples
Photography: Trever Clifford
Illustrator: Sue Cony
Props: Anne Sharples

Thanks to: Jessie Croome, Natalie Walsh, Juliet Taylor
and Christopher Liu: Elisabeth Smith Model Agency.

Printed and bound in Italy.

You will need to use scissors and glue to
make the props for your play. Always
make sure an adult is there to help you.

Use only water-based face paints and
make-up. Children with sensitive skin
should use make-up and face paints
with caution.

Contents

THE STORY OF SLEEPING BEAUTY

When a Bad Fairy puts a spell on Sleeping Beauty it looks as if all will be lost. The poor Princess must stay asleep for a hundred years, along with everyone else in her palace, until a handsome Prince rides by and saves the day with a kiss.

Choose a Part

This play is a story that you can read with your friends and perhaps even act out in front of an audience. You need up to four people. Before you start, choose which parts you would like to play.

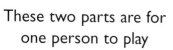
These two parts are for one person to play

Good Fairy
A kind fairy who makes good magic.

Sleeping Beauty
A beautiful young lady.

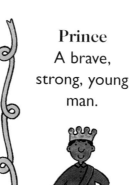

Prince
A brave, strong, young man.

Bad Fairy
A cackling witch who makes bad magic.

Storyteller
Someone who tells the tale.

How many people are going to take part?

If there are four people taking part, sit together so that you can all see the book.

If there are two or three people, share out the parts between you.

If you want to read the play on your own, use a different sounding voice for each part.

Reading the Play

Prince

Sleeping Beauty

Storyteller

Good Fairy

Bad Fairy

The play is made up of different parts. Next to each part there is a name and a picture. This shows who should be talking.

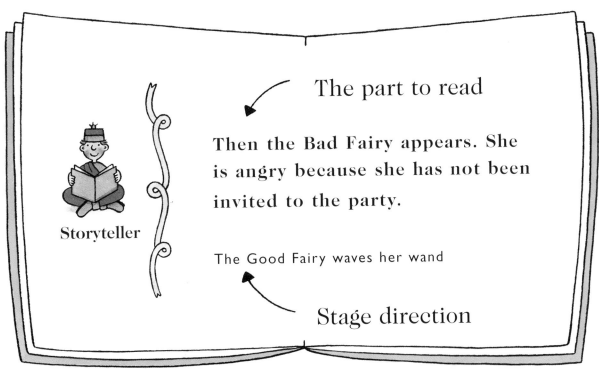

The part to read

Storyteller

Then the Bad Fairy appears. She is angry because she has not been invited to the party.

The Good Fairy waves her wand

Stage direction

In between the parts there are some stage directions. They are suggestions for things you might do, such as making a noise or miming an action.

Things to Make

Here are some suggestions for dressing the part.

THE BAD FAIRY: CLOTHES AND PROPS

Wear a black t-shirt or a leotard with black tights and shoes. Make a black skirt and wand. Mess up your hair and add some witchy facepaint.

Make a Black Skirt

You need:
- A black binliner
- 2 metres of string or black ribbon
- Scissors, ruler and glue
- Gold and blue paper

1. Snip raggedly along the bottom of the binliner to open it up.

2. Cut slits all around the top of the binliner, about 80mm down from the edge. Thread the string or ribbon through the slits.

3. Glue some blue and gold paper stars onto the skirt. Then pull the ends of the string tightly round your waist and tie them in a bow.

To disguise yourself at the spinning wheel (see page 16) wrap a shawl around you, or a blanket to look like a cloak.

Facepainting Ideas

Paint on green cheeks and a black wart. Put dark lipstick on and paint lots of big eyelashes or bushy eyebrows. Use hair gel to make your hair look wild and messy.

Make a Wand

You need:
- Black card
- Scissors and glue
- Pencil and ruler
- Glitter or shiny paint
- Saucer

1. Cut two long thin handles about the same size as a ruler, from the card. Glue them back-to-back to make your wand really strong.

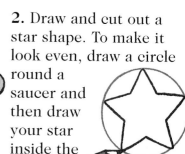

2. Draw and cut out a star shape. To make it look even, draw a circle round a saucer and then draw your star inside the circle.

3. Glue the star to the handle and decorate it with glitter or paint.

PRINCE: CLOTHES AND PROPS

Wear a grand crown and carry a sword to cut down the magic forest. Wear a dark blue shirt and trousers tucked into long blue socks. Put elegant cuffs around your knees and smart buckles on your shoes.

Make a Crown

You need:
- Shiny card (or plain card that you can paint yellow to look like gold)
- Glue, pencil and scissors
- Tape measure and ruler
- Coloured paper

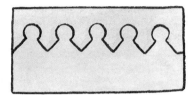

1. Draw a crown pattern on the back of the card. It can be as wide as you like with points along the top. It should be 75mm longer than the measurement around your head.

2. Cut out the shape and glue on scraps of coloured paper or screwed-up shiny sweet papers.

3. Put the two ends together, overlapping by about 40mm. Check it fits you and then tape or glue the ends together.

Cut out two card buckle shapes and fix them to your shoes with hair grips.

Make a sword out of card and paint it.

Make Knee Cuffs

You need:
- Black card or thick paper
- Hole punch
- String or shoe-laces
- Ruler, pencil and scissors
- Dinner plate

1. Draw part of the way round the dinner plate to make a curve with ends roughly 220mm apart.

2. Go round the curve measuring outwards by 10cm and making pencil marks all around it. Draw round the marks to make a bigger curve.

Make two cuffs the same.

3. Cut out the shape and punch holes in the corners. Thread string through the holes as shown and tie the cuffs together at the back of your legs.

GOOD FAIRY/SLEEPING BEAUTY: CLOTHES AND PROPS

Start off as the Good Fairy with a skirt just like the Bad Fairy's but made with a white binliner. Make a mask and wear a white t-shirt and white shoes. Wave a wand like the Bad Fairy's but decorated differently.

Change into Sleeping Beauty: Take off the mask and the white skirt. Put on a party dress or a net skirt and a pretty tiara.

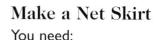

Make a Mask

You need:

- Some scrap paper and some stiff paper or thin card
- Scissors, pencil, ruler and glue
- Two long lengths of elastic
- Scraps of coloured paper or paint for decoration

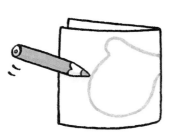

1. Practise first by cutting a rectangle of scrap paper 175mm by 75mm. Fold it in half and draw a round shape up to the fold, as shown.

2. Cut round the shape and unfold the paper. Hold it to your face to check the size and mark where the eyes should be. Cut them out.

3. Once you are happy with your practice mask, use it as a model to cut one from stiff paper. Decorate it how you like.

4. Make a hole in each side and knot elastic lengths through as shown. Tie them in a bow at the back.

Make a Net Skirt

You need:

- Piece of coloured net, 2m wide and as long as the measurement from your waist to your feet
- Scissors and ruler
- 2.5m of ribbon

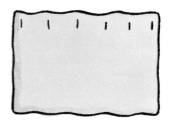

1. Lay the net flat and cut some slits all around the top, about 8cm down from the edge.

2. Thread the ribbon through the slots and pull the skirt tight around your waist. Tie the ends in a bow.

Stage and Sounds

Once you have read the play through you may want to perform it in front of an audience. If so, read through this section first. Rehearse the play, working out when you are going to come on and off stage and what actions you are going to perform.

PROPS

Wrap a doll in a sheet and use it to represent Sleeping Beauty at the Christening.

You will need a chair or stool for the Bad Fairy to sit on when she spins. She needs a shawl.

When Sleeping Beauty is asleep she could sit on a chair or lie on a duvet, or on some floor cushions.

The Bad Fairy needs to pretend to be sitting beside a spinning wheel. She could wrap a circle of lengths of wool around her hands to represent this.

Sleeping Beauty should practise pretending to prick a finger on an imaginary point.

SOUNDS

Riding noise:
As the Prince rides in, someone off-stage should make a clip-clopping noise by banging two coconut halves together or tapping a metal ruler on a door. If you have neither, experiment with different objects to get a good noise that the audience will hear.

LIGHTING

If you perform at night in a lit room, get an exciting effect by asking an assistant to flicker a torch quickly off and on again as the Bad Fairy does her spell.

REHEARSING

Rehearse the play before you ask someone to watch.

The Play

Storyteller

Once upon a time, long ago, a King and Queen lived in a beautiful palace surrounded by gardens. One day the Queen gave birth to a baby Princess. On the day of her Christening the King held a big party at the palace. The guest of honour was the Good Fairy, who gave the Princess some magic gifts.

The Storyteller points to the Good Fairy, who is holding a baby doll. The Fairy waves her wand over the doll.

Good Fairy

Sweet little one, I wish for you
Love and laughter ... Wisdom, too.
Beauty, kindness, gentle ways,
And happiness through all your days.

Storyteller

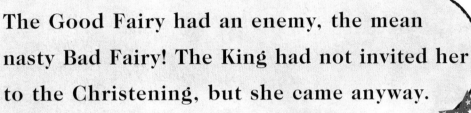

The Good Fairy had an enemy, the mean nasty Bad Fairy! The King had not invited her to the Christening, but she came anyway.

Bad Fairy

So! You're having a party and you didn't invite me! You're going to be very sorry.

Good Fairy

Please don't harm the Princess.

Bad Fairy

Shut up, goodie, goodie. I'm going to give the Princess a little magic gift of my own...

The Bad Fairy points her wand at the baby doll.

Bad Fairy

On your sixteenth birthday you will prick your finger on a spinning wheel. Then you will die!

The Bad Fairy laughs a nasty witch's laugh and disappears.

12

Storyteller

The Bad Fairy's spell was very powerful and it could not be completely broken. The Good Fairy could only change it.

The Good Fairy waves her wand over the baby doll.

Good Fairy

On the eve of your sixteenth birthday you will not die. Instead you will fall into a deep sleep for a hundred years.

COSTUME CHANGE

The Good Fairy should now change into her Sleeping Beauty outfit.

Storyteller

The King tried his best to stop the Bad Fairy getting her way. He had all the spinning wheels in his kingdom chopped up and burnt.

Storyteller

As the years passed, the Princess grew into a beautiful young woman.

The Storyteller points to Sleeping Beauty, who twirls around to show how beautiful she is.

Storyteller

On the eve of her sixteenth birthday she took a walk through the palace...

Sleeping Beauty

It's my birthday tomorrow! I'm so excited I can't sit still. Wait a minute ... I've never seen this door before. I wonder where it leads?

Make a creaking noise as Sleeping Beauty pretends to open the door.

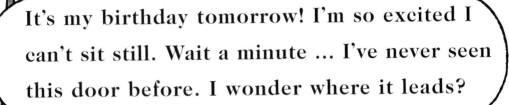

Storyteller

The door was a magic trick. Behind it were some magic stairs. At the top there was a magic room, and sitting in the magic room was the Bad Fairy!

The Bad Fairy sits on a chair with a shawl or cloak to hide her costume. She mimes spinning (see page 9).

Bad Fairy
(in old lady
voice)

Hello, dearie. Come in and see the lovely wool on the spinning wheel. Come closer ... closer ... Don't be scared.

Sleeping Beauty walks slowly towards the Bad Fairy, as if she is hypnotised.

Bad Fairy
(in old lady
voice)

Go on, dearie. Touch it ... Touch it ...

Sleeping Beauty reaches out and appears to touch a sharp point. She appears to prick her finger.

Sleeping Beauty

> **Aaaah! My finger!**

Bad Fairy

> **Now my evil spell is complete!**

The Bad Fairy throws off her shawl or cloak and disappears, laughing horribly.

Sleeping Beauty faints and lies still, in a deep sleep (see page 9 for prop idea).

Storyteller

The Bad Fairy's spell had come true, except for one thing. The Princess was not dead, just asleep. So was everyone else in the palace ... the servants, the footmen, the cooks, even the King and Queen.

Get everyone taking part to make snoring noises.

Storyteller

Time passed, day after day, year after year ... and a great thick forest grew up around the palace full of sleeping people. Exactly one hundred years later, a Prince came riding by.

Make a riding noise (see page 9).

Prince

What a strange place. It looks as if no-one has ever been able to get through the tangled trees. I think I'll try with my trusty sword.

The Prince raises his sword and appears to hack and chop his way through a forest. Then he stands back and gasps.

Prince

The trees are magic! They're moving apart for me. Wow! There's a palace in the middle!

19

Make a knocking noise on the back of your book.

Prince

> Hello, is anyone there...? No-one seems to be guarding the palace door. I'll go inside.

The other performers should make some snoring noises (off-stage if there is an audience).

Prince

> The palace guards are snoring! My goodness, there's a King and Queen fast asleep on their thrones! Now which way shall I go ...?

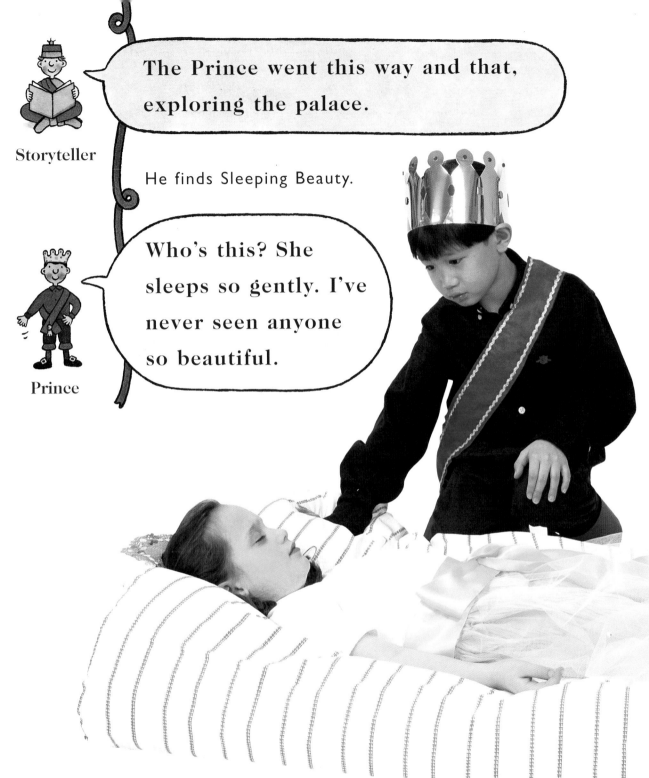

Storyteller

The Prince went this way and that, exploring the palace.

He finds Sleeping Beauty.

Prince

Who's this? She sleeps so gently. I've never seen anyone so beautiful.

The Prince bends over and kisses Sleeping Beauty, who slowly awakes.

Sleeping Beauty

What's happening? I must be dreaming. Who are you? Where am I?

Prince

Don't be frightened. I think you've woken from a deep, deep sleep.

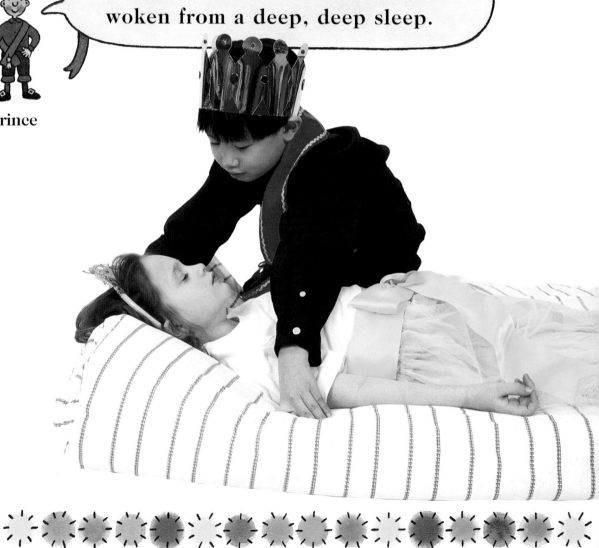

Sleeping
Beauty

I think I remember. There was a wicked fairy and a spinning wheel and bad magic ...

Prince

You're safe now, my beautiful lady. I will never let anyone harm you again.

Storyteller: Then everybody in the palace woke up. Life began once more, and very soon the Prince and Princess fell in love and were married.

Sleeping Beauty and the Prince hold hands.

Sleeping Beauty: The Bad Fairy's spell is broken.

Prince: Let's have a wedding day.

Storyteller: Now everyone is happy. We can end our little play.

Finish the play by bowing to each other or to the audience.